PUFFIN BOOKS

the battle of bubble and squeak

Philippa Pearce is the daughter of a miller and grew up in a mill house near Cambridge. The house, the river and the village feature in many of her best-loved children's books. She was educated at the Perse Girls' School in Cambridge and then at Girton College, Cambridge, where she read English and History. In addition to writing a great many books, she has also worked as a scriptwriter-producer for the BBC, a children's book editor, a book reviewer, a lecturer, a storyteller and as a freelance writer for radio and newspapers. Her now classic books for Puffin include Carnegie Medal winner *Tom's Midnight Garden, What the Neighbours Did and Other Stories, A Dog So Small* and her most recent novel, *The Little Gentleman. The Battle of Bubble and Squeak* won the Whitbread Award.

Books by Philippa Pearce

A DOG SO SMALL
THE BATTLE OF BUBBLE AND SQUEAK
THE LITTLE GENTLEMAN
THE ROPE AND OTHER STORIES
TOM'S MIDNIGHT GARDEN
THE WAY TO SATTIN SHORE
WHAT THE NEIGHBOURS DID

For younger readers

LION AT SCHOOL AND OTHER STORIES

Picture books

AMY'S THREE BEST THINGS

PHILIPPA PEARCE

the battle of bubble and squeak

ILLUSTRATED BY ANNABEL LARGE

PUFFIN

Penguin … 4, USA
Pengui… V 3B2
Penguin Irel… Books Ltd)
… Ltd)
Al… and Ltd)

Penguin Books Ltd, Registered Offices: 80 Strand, London WC2R ORL, England

www.penguin.com

First published by André Deutsch 1978
Published in Puffin Books 1980
Published in this edition 2005
007

Set in Bembo
Made and printed in England by Clays Ltd, St Ives plc

British Library Cataloguing in Publication Data
A CIP catalogue record for this book is available from the British Library

ISBN 0-141-32000-1

www.greenpenguin.co.uk

Penguin Books is committed to a sustainable future for our business, our readers and our planet. This book is made from Forest Stewardship Council™ certified paper.

ALWAYS LEARNING PEARSON

To Pam, not a gift but a tribute

CHAPTER I

The middle of the night, and everyone in the house asleep.

Everyone? Then what was that noise?

Creak! and then, after a pause, *Creak!* And then, *Creak!* And then, *Creak!* As regular as clockwork – but was this just clockwork? Behind the creaking, the lesser sound of some delicate tool working on metal.

The girls heard nothing. Amy Parker was so young that nothing ever disturbed her sleep. Peggy, too, slept soundly.

Sid Parker, their brother, heard in his dreams. He was the eldest by a little, and slept more lightly. Besides, he had been half expecting to hear something. He had dreaded to hear it. He came swimming up from the depths of his dreams to the surface: now he was wide awake, listening. *Creak!* he heard; and then *Creak!* . . . *Creak!* . . . *Creak!*

Sid broke into a sweat as he listened.

And their mother? Mrs Sparrow heard it. The noise woke her, as the crying of her children would have woken her. But this was someone else's job. She nudged her husband, the children's stepfather. She nudged and nudged until Bill Sparrow stirred, groaned. He had been dreaming of the garden: monster marrows, and runner beans that towered over their apple tree . . .

'Bill!' she whispered. 'Come on! Wake up!'

'Yes,' he said. 'Just a minute, and I'll do that.'

'Listen.'

Creak! And then, *Creak!* And then, *Creak!*

'Can't you hear it?'

'Yes.'

'What is it?'

'I don't know.'

'But it's in the house!'

'Yes, it is.'

'Downstairs!'

'Yes.'

'Bill! What are you going to do about it?'

He nearly said again, 'I don't know.' Then he pulled himself together. He tried hard to think clearly what he ought to do. First, he ought to wake up properly.

Then, he ought to get up. He ought to find out what was making the noise that bothered Alice so. That was it: find out.

'I'm getting up,' he said aloud. 'I'm going to find out about that row downstairs.'

He reached for the pencil-torch that Mrs Sparrow kept under the pillow. He wouldn't switch on the lights; he wouldn't even use the torch until he had to. He would surprise whatever it was. *Whoever* it was.

Burglars?

He ought to arm himself. A poker. But if you haven't open fires upstairs, you haven't pokers. He was in a bedroom: there wasn't a heavy spanner, or even an umbrella in that bedroom.

He paused as he was passing his wife's dressing-table. He picked up her heavy pot of cold cream.

'What *are* you doing, Bill?'

He pretended not to hear. If he had to do something about this noise, then he'd do it in his own way.

Softly he opened the bedroom door. Now that the door was open, he could hear it clearly: *Creak!* . . . And then, *Creak!* . . . And then, *Creak!*

Across the little landing were the doors of the children's bedrooms. The girls' bedroom door stood just ajar, as they liked it. Sid's door was also open – not ajar, but wide open. Bill Sparrow shone his torch in, cautiously, then boldly. The bed was empty.

He felt his way downstairs. He made for where the noise seemed to be coming from. He went from the foot of the stairs across to the kitchen. Much louder now: *Creak! . . . Creak! . . . Creak!* Clearer, too, the irregular sound of some kind of instrument that gnawed at metal.

And he became aware of a human undertone: a voice that whispered over and over again: 'Please, hush! . . . Please, hush! . . . Please! . . . Please! . . .'

'Sid,' said Bill Sparrow to himself, in wonder.

Across the kitchen to the walk-in larder. The larder door was only pulled to. Bill opened it gently, and shone his torch-beam inside.

Sid Parker crouched on the floor, in front of a cage in which two mouse-like creatures had frozen into stillness on the instant. One had been working a little treadmill fastened to the inside of a cage wall. The other had been gnawing at one of the bars of the cage.

The creatures had frozen. But Sid himself turned his head slowly, to see who shone the torch. He said, 'They're gerbils. My gerbils. Mine.'

Bill said: 'Those things?'

'Yes.'

'They were making that noise?'

'Yes. They're not supposed to be up and about at night. But they are.'

'Like me.'

But Sid rarely smiled at his stepfather's jokes. He asked, 'Did Mum hear?'

'You bet.'

The kitchen lights blazed on; the larder door was flung wide; Alice Sparrow stood in the doorway, like a flaming torch, leaving no corner unlit, catching in her glare her husband and her son. Catching them red-handed.

'Well!'

The gerbils had flashed into life. One whisked out of his treadmill; the other from his wire bar. They vanished into the hay that stuffed the inner box of their bedroom. The only indication of their presence in the cage was the drumming of tiny feet on the floor of the bedroom. The gerbils were drumming the alarm for extreme danger.

Sid had covered his face with his hands.

As for Bill Sparrow, he dropped the jar of cold cream. It would have smashed and splattered on the larder floor, but his wife caught it, under his arm, as it began its fall. She was expert at preventing mess.

Then the row began.

Alice Sparrow made the row. Bill Sparrow sat on the bread bin, leaning against the larder wall to recover himself. Sid now stood up in front of the gerbils' cage, meeting his mother's gaze, enduring it.

'It's no use your trying to hide them! I saw them!' cried Mrs Sparrow. 'Rats!'

'No,' said Sid. 'Gerbils.'

'Don't you contradict me at three in the morning,' said Mrs Sparrow. 'They're smelly little rats. Where've they come from?'

'The toolshed.'

'And none of your cheek! *Where've they come from?*'

'A boy at school gave them to me. Jimmy Dean's cousin. He gave them to me with the cage, last week. I put them in the shed. But then the nights began getting colder. I had to bring them indoors just for the night. I had to. They're used to hot deserts.'

'They go back to Jimmy Dean's cousin tomorrow without fail. Today, that is. How many times have I got to say that we're not having animals in this house? You've roller-skates and a camera and a transistor: what more do you want?'

'Two gerbils,' said Bill Sparrow in a mumble that no one heard.

Sid said: 'Mum, Jimmy Dean's cousin isn't at school any more. He's moved. Gone to Australia with his family. That's why he gave his animals away. So I can't give them back, Mum. Honest, I can't.'

She would not soften. 'Who gave them to Jimmy Dean's cousin, then?'

'No one. His dad bought them for him, in a Pet Department.'

She cackled with angry laughter. 'Some kids have fools for fathers. Where did you say he bought them?'

'The Pet Department in the Garden Centre.' Sid feared something – some plan – in his mother's mind. He was right.

She said: 'The Garden Centre isn't far. You can take those rats back.'

'They'll never take them back!' cried Sid.

'As a gift they will,' said his mother. 'They can sell them twice then, to two sets of fools.'

'Please, Mum!' He was almost crying.

'No! You take them back.'

'I won't!'

'Then I will. It'll make me late for work – and why I should have to carry a cageful of smelly rats! – But I'll take them.'

'Mum, they'll say they don't want any more gerbils, even as gifts. They'll have more than they can sell, anyway. Please, Mum, don't take them.'

'Rubbish!'

Bill Sparrow mumbled again. They paid no attention to him. Loudly, clearly, he repeated what he had said: 'I'll take them.'

CHAPTER 2

'What?'

'I'll take them,' Bill Sparrow said again.

Alice Sparrow looked at him with distrust; Sid with dislike.

'Why you?' asked his wife.

'I'll mind less than you do. I had white mice when I was a kid.'

'You keep quiet about that,' said Mrs Sparrow sharply.

'All right.'

'But you can take them. And mind you leave them at that Garden Centre! Sid, you go back to bed.'

Sid went.

That was the end of the row. The gerbils had crept out of their bedroom to her the end of it. One had climbed into the wheel again, and was treading it round: *Creak! . . . Creak! . . . Creak!*

'How am I going to endure that racket for the rest of the night?' asked Alice Sparrow.

'That wheel probably just needs a drop of oil,' said Bill. 'But, in the meantime, I think I could – yes, I can unscrew it from the cage wall.' He did not even need a tool; his fingers did the work. The wheel, released, fell over on to its side. The gerbils did not seem much put out.

'Come back to bed,' said Bill. He put an arm round his wife's shoulder. She shook it off irritably.

'You go up,' said Alice Sparrow. 'I must clear up the mess.' The gerbils had pushed some of their bedding through the bars of the cage, to fall on the larder floor. 'And I'll make myself some tea.'

Bill went.

Mrs Sparrow brushed up the mess from the larder floor. She noted that the gerbils made some more, at once. She seethed at that. But the kettle began to murmur. As it sang up and up towards boiling point, so she simmered down and down. She made the tea. While it brewed, she looked into the larder again. More mess on the floor, of course. And the gerbils were gnawing metal again; but the gnawing by itself was not noisy. Nor – Alice Sparrow sniffed the air – did gerbils smell. Nor were they really like rats, to look at. Their tails were furry, for one thing.

On the other hand, she didn't like animals, had never liked animals, and never would like animals. It was bad luck that the three children had not taken after her in this. They were like their father, who had died soon after Amy was born. No doubt, if he had lived, the house would have swarmed with cats, dogs, rabbits, guinea-pigs, hamsters, budgerigars, and canaries in yellow clouds. What would *she* have been like, then? Alice drank her tea slowly and thought all kinds of things.

She poured a second cup of tea and took it upstairs with her. Sid's bedroom door was shut. She opened it quietly and looked in. She was pretty sure he was awake, but his back was towards the door, his shoulder hunched high like a wall. There seemed no point in saying good night to that shoulder. She closed the door again.

She went into the girls' room. As she stood over her, Peggy stirred.

'Mum? Something happened?'

'Nothing important, love.'

Peggy slept again.

As for Amy, she was deeply asleep, as usual. Her mother knelt by her bed, put her arms round her, hugged her. There was little fear of disturbing Amy. She hugged her, kissed her, buried her face in the warmth of sleeping little girl. She knelt there for minutes.

When at last she left the child, her second cup of tea was almost cold.

In her own bedroom: 'Bill!' she whispered.

But Bill Sparrow was already asleep.

Alice Sparrow's last thought before sleep was that Peggy and Amy need never know that gerbils had been in the house. Better so.

At breakfast-time next morning, there was no mention at all of the gerbils, unless you count Mrs Sparrow's saying to her husband: 'Don't forget.'

'No,' said Bill.

And once, when Peggy was going to the larder for more cornflakes, her mother said – to Peggy's surprise – 'Sit still. I'll get them.'

And when Mrs Sparrow was getting Amy into her anorak, Amy said: 'What's that noise?'

'There isn't a noise,' said her mother.

Amy said, 'A grinding sort of little noise in the larder, like tiny little people gnawing their own knives and forks. Bill hears it.'

'He doesn't,' said her mother.

'Why are you afraid of them?' asked Amy.

'This isn't the time of day for fairy tales,' said her mother.

Sid sat silent and rather pale, eating his breakfast, looking at nobody.

By eight o'clock on a weekday morning the house was beginning to empty itself. The first to go were Peggy and Amy. Friends called for them on their way to school. Peggy's friend was Dawn Mudd. Mrs Sparrow had once said sarcastically that she ought to have been Sunset Mudd: she was the last – after a long gap in time – of a very large family. She was already an aunt several times over, and her mother was always knitting baby clothes for grandchildren. Dawn Mudd was small, with straight red hair and gimlet eyes.

Peter Peters came with Dawn Mudd. ('They must have been at their wits' end for names, when *he* was born,' Mrs Sparrow said.) He was in the same infant class as Amy.

After these four had left the house, it was Bill Sparrow's turn. He bicycled to work in the warehouses of the General Supply Company. This morning he left with a gerbil cage and gerbils in his large bicycle basket.

Then Mrs Sparrow left. At one time she had made a point of leaving last, so that she could lock up behind her; but that had always put her in a rush. (She had a job in the offices of the same General Supply Company: full time during school term; mornings only in the holidays.) Now Sid had started at secondary school, and was old enough to be entrusted with responsibility. He locked up.

By half past eight, on any weekday, the house had been emptied of life.

This morning, already, they had all gone, except for Sid.

As usual, his mother had washed up and tidied before going off. The kitchen was spick and span. Sid stood in the middle of it, in no great hurry yet. The school bus-stop was just at the end of the road.

He stood in the middle of the kitchen and shut his eyes. He imagined Bill Sparrow riding along with the gerbil cage in his bicycle basket, the gerbils keeping their footing with difficulty, like tiny sailors in a rough sea.

Round Sid, the house was still and silent. It waited for him and his imaginings to go. He was the last living thing.

He kept his eyes shut. He said aloud slowly: 'I wish this house would smash. I wish it would crash and smash and fall on me. Brick by brick by brick. All the bricks in this house can fall on me and kill me. The Council can have it back again, all rubble. Me under the rubble.'

He stopped speaking.

Deep silence.

The house waited, bored.

He opened his eyes. Everything as before, clean and tidy.

He walked into the walk-in larder and stood looking around. There was not a trace of where the gerbil cage had been. His mother had swept up the last wisp of bedding from the floor after Bill had taken the cage out to his bicycle.

He thought again of Bill on his bicycle. He would be within sight of the Garden Centre by now.

He looked round the larder. In perfect order.

There was a small bowl of dripping on the shelf – bacon fat from breakfast, still partly runny. He took it up in two hands, testing its weight. He held it in front of him, but high – high –

Carefully, he dropped it.

The bowl smashed and the fat splattered everywhere.

He was frightened at the mess he had made.

He left the larder door ajar.

He opened the kitchen window a little, and left it like that.

He gathered together his school things and rushed out of the house. He locked the door behind him and kept the key in his hand. He ran down the front path, along the road, and up Mrs Pring's front path to her little bungalow. He shot the key through the letterbox with a yell ('Key as usual, Mrs Pring!'), leapt over one of the Pring cats as it ambled round the corner of the house, and was out in the road again, running. He caught up with Jimmy Dean, bound for the same school bus. He was thinking of Bill Sparrow again, although he would rather not have done.

Jimmy heard him coming and waited.

'Hi, Sid!'

'Hi, Jimmy!' Certainly Bill would have reached the entrance to the Garden Centre by now.

'Saw the match last night?'

'You bet!' Would Bill have turned into the entrance? Would he be dismounting? Lifting the gerbil cage from the bicycle basket?

'What a smash-up!'

'I'll say!'

They walked together the rest of the way to the stop for the school bus, talking football. Jimmy Dean was a football friend.

All that day the Council house where the Sparrows

and Parkers lived stayed empty, without the disturbance of life; spick and span – except, of course, for the larder. For a while, bacon fat crept slowly down the walls where it had splashed, and over the floor. Then it congealed.

The family began coming back at the end of the afternoon. Usually Peggy and Amy, accompanied to the front gate by their friends, were first. They let themselves in with the key from old Mrs Pring. But today Bill Sparrow with his own key overtook them before they reached Mrs Pring's. So they all came home with him – all of them.

Sid came next.

Today Mrs Sparrow was the last to arrive. She had had household shopping to do on the way home.

Mrs Sparrow walked in through the back door into the kitchen, and immediately Sid darted out of the larder at her.

'It's all right, Mum! Honest, it is! I've almost finished!'

'What's all right? What is it?'

'There was a bowl of dripping in the larder and it must have got knocked off the shelf –'

'*What!*'

'The larder door hadn't been shut, and the kitchen window was open –'

'*I* never left the kitchen window open!'

'– So it must have been a cat, mustn't it? One of Mrs Pring's. But I've been cleaning the mess up. Honestly. I've nearly finished.'

She looked into the larder and groaned. 'It's not nearly right, Sid. Still, you're a good boy.'

Sid reddened. He said: 'I'm sorry about the mess, and the work there still is.'

His mother said wearily: 'Get that cat to say it's sorry; not you. Not your fault.' She looked around. 'No one put the kettle on?'

'We forgot . . .'

She began to notice other things out of the ordinary. Shrill voices and laughter came from the living-room.

'Who's there? That's not just Peggy and Amy. They've got the other two as well! Why haven't those two gone home to their own teas?'

She marched out of the kitchen to the living-room and flung the door open. She was right. Round the table, leaning excitedly over it, were Peggy, Amy, Dawn Mudd and Peter Peters. At first Mrs Sparrow did not understand what she was looking at. The table was covered with long tubes made of rolled up newspaper. As she stared, there was a scrabbling and a shaking inside one of the tubes, and then a tiny head with pop eyes looked out at one end.

'That's one of those gerbil-things,' Mrs Sparrow said in the voice of a sleepwalker.

The gerbil seemed not to like her tone, for it withdrew into the tube again. Meanwhile, another gerbil sat up on its hind-legs behind another tube, on which it rested one front paw, as if to begin public speaking. It held its other paw against its white shirt-front.

The gerbil cage stood, open, at the back of the table, under the window.

In an easy chair, to one side of the fire, sat Bill Sparrow with the evening paper.

'Bill!'

He said, 'Sid was quite right. The Pet Department wouldn't take them at any price. I had to bring them home again.'

Amy rushed at her mother, to clasp her round her knees. 'Oh, Mum, they're lovely – lovely! And Sid's been letting us play with them while he cleared up for you in the larder!'

Dawn Mudd had picked up a gerbil by its tail and was looking intently at its underside – or trying to. The gerbil was trying to bite Dawn Mudd. Dawn said, 'Mrs Sparrow, I can't make out what sex they are. But if they're different sexes, you'll be in luck. They'll mate, and have babies.'

'Babies! Babies! Babies!' crowed Amy.

CHAPTER 3

In the circumstances, surely Mrs Sparrow could not go on saying that she would not have gerbils in the house! But she did. As soon as she could think of a way, she was going to get rid of them.

In the meantime, there they were.

As long as they were there, the gerbils belonged to Sid. But, from that very first afternoon, Peggy was the one who loved them. Sid would be doing his homework, or out playing football, or just watching television. ('Why does he want them then, when he seems hardly to bother with them?' his mother asked his stepfather. 'I remember my white mice,' said Bill

Sparrow.) While Sid busied himself with these things, Peggy sat with her head between her hands, her elbows on the table, watching the gerbils as they flickered to and fro in their cage.

Sometimes – for Sid trusted her – she would carefully undo the fastening of the cage door and take out a gerbil, fastening the door again with equal care. She would let the gerbil pour itself from her right hand into her left, and then her right hand was ready to receive it again, and then her left, and then her right again, in an endless handy-dandy. The softness and lightness and warmth of the little, quick-moving body against her fingers and in the palms of her hands delighted Peggy.

She always knew which gerbil she was playing with. Sid had named the two of them (as was his right) after one of his favourite foods. Cold boiled cabbage and potato, fried up with cold meat or sausage, did not seem in itself at all gerbil-like; but the name sounded right: bubble-and-squeak.

Bubble and Squeak.

But which was Bubble, which Squeak? Even sharp-eyed Dawn Mudd couldn't always spot the darker brindle that (Peggy said) marked Bubble. Even Dawn couldn't always swear which gerbil had the longer tail by (Peggy estimated) just three millimetres. Dawn complained that the gerbils whisked about so in their cage.

But Peggy always knew which was which.

'Do you think they know their own names?' asked

Dawn Mudd. And Amy chirruped through the bars: 'Bubble and Squeak! Bubble and Squeak!'

Peggy ran her fingernail across the front of the cage. Both gerbils sat up on their hind-legs, attentive. Between the finger-tips of her other hand Peggy held a peanut. One of the gerbils did a sudden scurry to the cage front. 'Squeak!' Peggy whispered. 'Come on, Squeak – Squeak – Squeak!' She offered the peanut through the bars. Squeak took it and at once veered away. Turning the nut round and round between his paws, he began to nibble at it with great rapidity.

'Dear Bubble, wouldn't you like a nut too?' This was Amy.

The other gerbil had already moved up to the bars, and took his nut.

'He's the quiet one,' said Peggy.

'He?' said Dawn Mudd, raising a subject that interested her.

'Well,' said Peggy, 'they must be the same sex, because Jimmy Dean's cousin said they'd never had babies. And if they're the same sex, *I* think they're boys. Bubble and Squeak are boy's names.'

That was that.

Sid may not have loved his gerbils in the way that Peggy did, but he was conscientious about them. He changed their food and water daily, and cleaned out their cage every weekend. He exercised them often. What they seemed to enjoy was the freedom of a limitless plain – the living-room table would do – with a great many tunnels. To begin with, the children made the tunnels out of newspapers rolled up, with rubber bands to keep the rolling-up in place. Then they began to collect the cardboard inner tubes of toilet rolls from the lavatory and of kitchen rolls from the kitchen. The longer tubes were kept for the table; the shorter ones went straight into the cage.

Besides using the tubes as runways, the gerbils gnawed them to bits. If they didn't gnaw cardboard, they gnawed the bars of the cage or of the restored treadmill. The cardboard they gnawed filled the cage with cardboard crumbs, and the crumbs pushed themselves out through the bars of the cage on to the table or the floor; so did the gerbil bedding. Someone had to clear up the mess. After that first night's experience, Mrs Sparrow refused to do any more clearing up after gerbils. Sid did it. He used the vacuum cleaner regularly nowadays. He did not object. He rather enjoyed the job of emptying the cleaner. Once it went wrong, and he mended it.

'You can't say he doesn't work at it,' said Bill Sparrow. 'You might do worse than keep those gerbils, you know.'

'You're soft,' said Alice Sparrow. 'I don't like them. I don't *trust* them.'

It turned out that she was right not to trust them.

The gerbil cage was kept on the living-room table, until the table was needed. Then Sid or Peggy would lift the cage on to the wide window-sill. When the table was clear again, the cage was put back. But sometimes, of course, the children forgot to do that. It did not seem to matter much if the gerbils stayed on the window-sill, anyway. There was even room, after dark, to draw the curtains across the window, between the back of the cage and the window itself.

The curtains were rather handsome scarlet ones that Mrs Sparrow had made herself. When they were drawn behind the cage, their folds brushed against the bars at the back.

One morning Mrs Sparrow was down first, as usual, to get breakfast ready. She had raised the blind in the hall, she had brought the milk in from the doorstep, she had gone into the living-room to draw the curtains back –

There was a kind of screech from downstairs, and then the repeated screaming of 'Sid! Sid! Sid!'

It was frightening.

In his school trousers and his pyjama top, Sid flew downstairs. His mother met him at the bottom of the stairs. Tears were streaming down her cheeks; she also looked unspeakably angry. 'Come and see what your – your THINGS have done!'

She dragged him into the living-room. The room was still in semi-darkness because the curtains had not yet been drawn back. But the gloom was shot by strong beams of light coming through two large ragged holes in the curtains. The holes were just behind the cage, and by the light through them Sid could see that the inside of the gerbil cage was littered with scraps and crumbs of scarlet. One gerbil, sitting up watchfully, seemed to be wiping its mouth free of a scarlet thread.

'They've eaten my best curtains,' said Mrs Sparrow.

Peggy had followed Sid, and now Amy and Bill Sparrow were crowding to see, Amy holding tight to Bill.

Amy peeped and peered. 'I didn't know gerbils ate curtains.'

'They don't *eat* them,' said Peggy. 'They just gnaw at them.'

'They've ruined them,' said Mrs Sparrow.

'Can't you mend them?' asked Bill Sparrow.

'Can't *I* mend them!'

'I'll mend them,' said Sid. 'I'll draw the edges of the holes together. I saw you mending that tear in my duffle coat, when it had caught on the barbed wire. I'll buy red cotton exactly to match, and I'll mend it. Peggy'll help me, won't you, Peg?'

'Yes,' said Peggy; 'but – but –'

'But you can't,' said their mother. 'Your duffle coat was just torn: there was nothing missing. These curtains have been *gnawed away*. Big bits are missing, all chewed up at the bottom of those wretched creatures' cage.'

'I'll do something, Mum!' cried Sid. 'I could buy some more of the red stuff to patch the holes with. I've pocket money saved up. I could buy you new curtains. Mum, I tell you what –'

'No,' said his mother, 'I'm not thinking of the curtains now.'

'But, Mum, listen –'

'No,' said his mother, 'no, no, NO! Not another day in this house, if I can help it! They go!'

'But, Mum –'

'THEY GO!'

She would listen to no more from any of them.

That day (as her family discovered only later) Mrs Sparrow went out of her way to work to call at the newsagent's. They kept a *Wanted* and *For Sale* notice board in their window. The board was covered with postcard notices which people paid to be pinned up there for a week, or two weeks, or – rarely – three.

Mrs Sparrow paid in advance for three weeks, and her notice went up:

FREE

TWO VERY ATTRACTIVE GERBILS

WITH CAGE, FOOD AND BEDDING.

And Mrs Sparrow added at the bottom her own name and the address.

CHAPTER 4

The advertisement worked. The very next evening people called.

Mrs Sparrow had hoped for this, of course, and she was determined that no one in her family should spoil her chances. She had arranged to be home early from work, before any of the others. Any ring or knock at the front door that evening would be answered by her, and by her alone.

But if Sid were in by the time any caller came . . . She worried about how she could possibly get the gerbils out of the house, to new owners, without Sid's knowledge. She did not fear that Sid could stop her handing them over; but might he follow the new owners to their home – oh, then what?

She planned to get Sid upstairs for the evening. She spread dressmaking things all over the big table in the living-room. (The gerbils went on to the window-sill. No point in worrying about the curtains any more, now.) She would do dressmaking all evening. They would think it peculiar, but she didn't mind that. She would give Bill and Amy and possibly Peggy a snack tea by the fire. She would make some good sandwiches and a mug of tea for Sid to take upstairs to his room. Sid could do his homework on his table there.

But what about Peggy? And might Peggy tell Sid?

She was getting the sewing machine on to the table, and worrying about Peggy, when the front door bell went.

There were two little boys there. Brothers, by their appearance. They seemed to be between Peggy and Amy in age. They said they had come for the free gerbils.

'Wait there!' cried Mrs Sparrow. She darted back into the living-room, snatched up the cage, an unopened packet of gerbil food and the plastic bag of bedding, and was back on the doorstep again. 'You'd better get home with them at once. Quick! Don't stop to talk to anybody on the way. Don't stop at all.'

The little boys were delighted, but flustered. They were afraid the excited lady might change her mind. They hurried to the gate, carrying the cage between them.

'Cross the road and walk back on the other side!' Mrs Sparrow called after them. She had just remembered that the Parker children always walked home on this side of the road.

'Why?' asked one brother.

'Never you mind!'

They were opening the front gate.

'Wait!' called Mrs Sparrow.

'Yes?'

She had felt an unexpected spasm of concern for the little creatures in the cage. She took a duster down to the gate and draped it over the cage. It would protect the inmates from the cold. (It would also disguise the cage a little.) 'You know how to look after these gerbil-things?' Mrs Sparrow asked.

'Oh, yes! We had gerbils once. We had a gerbil *farm*.'

They hurried through the gate and across the road and away.

Boys, cage, and gerbils – they had vanished.

Mrs Sparrow went in again and shut the front door. She went into the kitchen and sat down on a chair, feeling a little faint. She glanced at the clock. The children were certainly on their way home now.

Nearly home . . .

Soon they would be walking up the last stretch of road, as the two brothers with the cage would be walking down it. On opposite sides of the road, it was true; but would that help much? Would Sid notice the cage? Or Peggy? Or Amy? Would they cross the road to talk to the two boys? Would the boys allow themselves to be talked to – their cage to be examined? Would Sid or Peggy recognize the gerbils? Oh, no, no, no!

Mrs Sparrow groaned aloud.

There was nothing more that she could do.

She cleared her dressmaking things from the table and began getting tea for them all.

Meanwhile, just as she had supposed, her children were walking up the road, drawing closer and closer to the two little boys, a gerbil cage swinging between them, who were going down it on the other side.

Today Sid, with Jimmy Dean, came first. They happened to be fighting the whole way. For a great deal of the time, Sid's head was under Jimmy's arm. He saw nothing.

The elder girls, when they came, were talking gossip about other girls; and Amy was listening to them intently. Only little Peter Peters, trailing behind, saw the boys on the other side of the road. He saw the cage, even under the duster.

'Look!' he said.

But no one looked.

It was some time after they had all got home that Sid, in the living-room, realized: 'Where are my gerbils?'

His mother clenched her fists under her overall, cleared her throat, and told him. The telling took a little while, because Sid knew nothing of the advertisement in the first place.

Sid listened. He stood quite still and silent, staring at his mother, expressionless.

Peggy also listened. At the end, with deceptive mildness, she asked: 'Who were the boys? Where do they live?'

But Mrs Sparrow was not deceived. 'Oh, no, you don't!' she said. 'I don't know who they are, and I don't know where they live. And they'll be far away by now. Probably home already.'

Sid turned round and rushed out of the house.

'Sid! Sid!' called his mother.

Peggy sat down on the bottom step of the stairs and buried her face in her crossed arms.

Bill Sparrow was pushing his bike through the front gate. 'Here!' he grumbled, as Sid shoved past him.

Sid began running down the road.

Amy had followed him out. She came up to Bill Sparrow. Her eyes were very wide. 'The gerbils have gone,' she said. 'Mum's given Bubble and Squeak to two bad boys. They've stolen them.'

'Oh,' said Bill Sparrow. She followed him while he put his bike away. She touched his left hand with her right one – it was her signal. He stuck out a finger. She wrapped her hand round it, and they walked indoors together.

'Sid's gone out without his tea or his anorak or anything,' said Mrs Sparrow as soon as she saw her husband. In spite of the gerbils, she did not look triumphant.

'Sid'll be back,' said Bill Sparrow. 'We might as well have tea.'

'Will he come back with Bubble and Squeak?' asked Amy.

'No,' said her mother.

'Where's Peggy?' asked Amy.

'She's upstairs. She doesn't want any tea. *And don't ask any more questions.*' As his wife stood making the tea, Bill Sparrow massaged her shoulders. He did this when she complained of back-ache.

By the end of tea, Sid had not come back.

'Bill, aren't you going after him?'

'No, because he'll come back on his own.'

But he didn't.

Dusk had fallen. Mrs Sparrow went out into the hall and brought her coat into the living-room and began putting it on.

'All right,' said Bill Sparrow, 'I'll go.'

He put on his raincoat – it was a damp night – and got on his bicycle. He cycled slowly from the estate into the centre of the village. That was the obvious way for Sid to have gone. If the two boys were unknown on the estate, then it was likely that they lived in the village. But there was no sign of Sid. In the centre of the village, everything was shut up. Nobody in the streets.

Bill Sparrow turned and went home.

'Hasn't he turned up yet?' he asked his wife.

'No.'

He went round to the Deans', but Sid was not there. Nor had Jimmy Dean's father seen him on the estate. (Mr Dean always exercised their dog at that time of evening.) He asked old Mrs Pring if she had seen Sid. She and her cats kept a pretty close watch, through net curtains, on who came and who went. But she had not seen Sid. He even called at the Mudds', to see if by any chance Sid were there. He was not, but Dawn Mudd put on her coat and came back with him. She seemed positively to have sharpened her nose for this mystery, Bill Sparrow thought.

'I shall go to the police,' said Mrs Sparrow flatly.

'But he hasn't run away,' said Bill Sparrow. 'He just hasn't come home yet.'

'That's why I shall go to the police.'

'Don't, Alice! Let me have another try.'

Dawn Mudd was listening intently.

'And where are you going to have another try?' Mrs Sparrow asked.

'I'll go somewhere I haven't been before.'

He did not know where. But Dawn Mudd followed him to the front door: 'There's a place he might be . . .'

'Where?'

'It's confidential. Sid knows he can't find Bubble and Squeak. He's given *that* up. So he's not coming home because he feels awful. He's just gone somewhere to feel awful in.'

'Well?'

'An awful place. There's one we found last summer. We tried to have a picnic there – Peggy and me and Amy and Sid and Jimmy Dean. It's a straggly little wood, away from people and houses altogether. In the opposite direction from the village. You go up a little hill and down a little hill, and then –'

'I know,' said Bill Sparrow. 'Then it's on the left.'

'It's boggy where you go in. Somebody's driven an old car round the boggy bit and into the wood and dumped it. It's not nice there.'

'I'll go,' said Bill.

On his bike again, he took the road that led away from the village and the estate. He came to an end of the street lighting. To the end of speed restrictions on traffic. Up a dark hill; down a dark hill; and there, to one side of the road, on the left, was a deeper black than the darkness round it: the wood.

He got off his bicycle and leant it against a gate that seemed to mark an entrance into the wood. He climbed the gate slowly, walked away from it into the wood, skirted the boggy patch, and stopped.

As Dawn Mudd had said, in no way was this a nice wood.

The outer parts of the wood seemed haunted by the sharp-edged, painful ghosts of people's worn out metal-ware. When he moved again, he trod on something that thereupon rose up out of the wintry undergrowth like a snake rearing to strike: an old bicycle mudguard. Soon he saw ahead of him, like some sunken hovel, the dumped car that Dawn Mudd had mentioned. All the doors were off. The sickening smell of rot and rust from inside made him certain that Sid was not sheltering there.

He penetrated farther into the wood – farther, probably, than most people bothered to go who were dumping rubbish. He could feel round him that the trees were growing closer together. The brambles seemed to spring at least waist high. They seemed deliberately to tear at him. He tripped on a low one, and put his hand out to steady himself on an upright darkness that must be a tree. He felt the tree trunk quite solid under his hand, but then it seemed to move away from him. In terror he stumbled forward. He recovered himself, and realized that this really was only a tree: it had died, or been felled by the wind, but could not fall because of closely surrounding trees. It was supported by its companions, dead on its feet, the corpse of a tree.

He wished that he had brought his torch with him into this wood. Really, he could see nothing; and he could hear nothing except his own crashing about and his own uneven breathing. When he stood still and listened to his breathing, it struck him as sounding like the breathing of a frightened man.

He tried to quiet himself, so that he could listen for noises outside himself, beyond himself. He strained his ears to hear the faintest, most distant sound in the wood, that might be Sid.

But Sid might not be here after all. It was ridiculous of him to have paid any attention to Dawn Mudd. What could she *know*?

Or, if Sid had come here, he might have gone by now. He might have left the wood as Bill himself had entered it, under cover of all the noise that Bill had been making.

There might be no Sid. He might be quite alone in the wood.

Then, much, much closer than he could ever have

expected it, came Sid's voice. It sounded thin and hard. Very unpleasant.

'I've got a knife,' said Sid.

'A *knife*?' His voice was dying in his throat.

'Who is it, then?'

'Me. Bill.'

Suddenly Sid was at his elbow, ordinary again, but cross. 'I thought it was someone else.'

'Who?'

'I don't know. Oh,' – he sounded too careless – 'the kind of man who'd choose to go into the middle of a wood like this, all alone, after dark. Or someone who'd watched me go in. Waited. Followed me . . .'

'Well,' said Bill. 'I hadn't much choice in coming. Your mum sent me out.'

Sid was furious. 'Can't you do anything on your own? Do you always have to do what *she* says?'

'No,' said Bill, 'but mostly.'

'It's not your fault my gerbils didn't go long ago. You took them to be sold. *Offered* to take them.'

'And I brought them back.'

'You had to.'

'No.'

There was a pause. Sid said resentfully: 'What do you mean, "No"?'

'The Garden Centre would have taken them back all right. But, in the end, I didn't ask them to.'

A much longer pause. Sid had to make sure: 'Didn't ask them to?'

'No. I just brought the cage back, without going into

the Pet Department at all.' He couldn't help adding: 'Don't tell your mum.'

A long, long pause. Then Sid laughed. Then said: 'Well, they're gone now.'

'Yes, but I suppose . . .'

'What?'

'You might get two more.'

'You mean, in spite of Mum? *Against* Mum?'

'She'd have to be talked round.'

'And who'd do that?'

'Well, I'd try.'

'Why?'

'I'm –' Bill Sparrow hesitated. 'I'm your stepfather. And, when I was your age, I had white mice.'

Sid moved away, but not deeper into the wood. He was making for the road. Bill Sparrow followed him closely.

As they came out from the gloom of the trees, Bill saw that Sid really did have a knife – a big thing, with a wicked big blade, open. He had been hacking at brambles and branches with it, as he went. Now he was snapping it shut.

'Where did you get that knife?' Bill said.

'I stole it.'

'*Stole* it?'

'Out of Mum's chest of drawers. Top left-hand drawer. It was my dad's pruning knife.'

'If you like, I'll put it back for you.' Sid gave it to him. 'And you know, your mum's worrying about you. Take my bike, and get home quickly.'

Sid said, 'I trod in something – ugh! – as I was going into the wood.'

'You stink,' Bill agreed. 'Get it off now. I'll go on.'

Bill Sparrow left Sid working away at the side of his shoe in the grass. He set off walking. Half-way down the hill, Sid passed him on the bike. 'Hi!' he called, as he flew on.

By the time Bill Sparrow got home, Sid was eating his tea. Dawn Mudd, having seen him arrive, had gone.

Mrs Sparrow was happy. She brewed a fresh pot of tea for her husband, and fussed over him, as she had already fussed over Sid. No mention was made of gerbils until after the children had gone to bed. Then, 'It turns out there's quite a demand for gerbils, after all,' said Mrs Sparrow. 'While you were out, someone else came asking about the advert.'

'I've been thinking about gerbils and white mice,' said Bill Sparrow. He cleared his throat.

'Not tonight,' said his wife. 'We've had enough tonight. Tomorrow, if you like.'

But on the next night there was no need for discussion. Three more sets of people called on Mrs Sparrow because of her gerbil advertisement. Mrs Sparrow told the first two, blithely, that they were much too late.

The third set of people were the two little boys who had taken the gerbils in the first place, and their mother. Their mother carried the cage with Bubble and Squeak in it. She was unpleasantly polite. 'We have come to return your kind gift,' she said. 'In my opinion, parents should always be consulted before children are given presents which parents may not want. We have had animals similar to these in the past. They bred. We don't want them again. *Any more than you seem to want them.*'

The gerbils in their cage, the bedding, what remained of the food – all were dumped on the doorstep. Peggy, who had come behind her mother, stooped, reached past her, and brought everything indoors again.

The mother was marching her two little boys back through the front gate and away. 'Here!' called Mrs Sparrow. But the other woman paid no attention.

Behind her, indoors, Mrs Sparrow could hear the rest of her family welcoming home dear Bubble and Squeak. She could not bear it. She ran frantically down to the front gate. 'HERE!' she shouted.

But, of course, everything was useless.

She went slowly back up the path, in through the front door, shut it behind her. The living-room door was shut, but she could hear the sounds of delight behind it. She opened that door, stood in the doorway, looked.

A gerbil festival was going on.

Sid lay on the floor, and Peggy and Amy were each in charge of a gerbil. They were feeding Bubble and Squeak into the sleeves of Sid's jacket and into his trouser-legs. Tails disappeared; there were scurryings; uncontrollable gigglings were tickled out of Sid; pop-eyed gerbil faces popped out of trouser-ends, sleeve-ends; there were two gerbils – there were twenty gerbils; Sid was gerbil-infested.

Everyone was laughing, not loudly, but softly, affectionately.

And Bill stood over them, laughing too.

Mrs Sparrow stood in the doorway, and looked. They never noticed her. She backed out and slammed the door – but perhaps they never noticed that either?

She went into the kitchen and sat down. She felt like screaming and screaming; but she knew that she never screamed.

CHAPTER 5

That evening Alice Sparrow hardly spoke to her family.

That night she hardly slept.

The next morning she was up very early, before anyone else. For one thing, it was the day for the dustbins. She busied herself indoors and out.

At one point, 'That's that,' she said, brushing her hands together smartly.

Later, nearly at breakfast-time, there was a ring at the doorbell. She answered it. One of the dustmen stood there. He held the gerbil cage in front of him. 'Missus,' he said, 'you can't do this. There's something alive in here.'

Mrs Sparrow had thought she was still the only one downstairs, but Amy had come behind her. Amy looked past her. She saw the dustman and the cage he held. She looked past him. She saw the huge van that had drawn up just past the front gate. She saw the open back of the van and the great fangs that closed slowly and opened . . . and closed . . . and opened . . .

She began to scream.

Mrs Sparrow took the cage from the man. She shut the front door on him and on the sight of the fangs.

Amy's screaming turned to crying. She cried as if her heart would break.

Mrs Sparrow took the cage into the kitchen and put it safely on the table there. Bubble and Squeak came out and pottered about, unaware of drama. Mrs Sparrow sat down and took Amy on to her knee. Amy, still crying, fought her.

'Amy,' her mother said. 'Listen. Listen, Amy. I didn't mean them to go into the van. Truly. I put them on top of the dustbin, not inside. Truly. I thought one of the dustbin-men might have a little girl that liked gerbils.'

Amy wailed: 'I'm a little girl that likes gerbils! I love Bubble and Squeak!'

She still cried, but she was beginning to allow her mother to cuddle her. This was as her mother talked to her, coaxed her, promised her. Mrs Sparrow found herself promising that – No, she wouldn't send Bubble and Squeak away. She would never send them away.

As she was promising, Sid and Peggy walked into the kitchen; and Bill Sparrow was just behind them.

They all heard her promising.

CHAPTER 6

The night after the dustbin morning was a bad one. Everyone was asleep when the screaming began. At first it was difficult to know who was screaming.

Amy, still deeply asleep, screamed and screamed.

She was having a nightmare: tiny trickles of blood were oozing from between the black bars of a cage. The trickles widened and deepened into streams, into rivers, into torrents and seas. At last Amy was sinking and drowning in the rushing and roaring tides of hateful oceans.

She woke everyone with her screaming; lastly, herself. Her mother had to spend a long time with her, cuddling and coaxing her all over again, calming her, reassuring her with yet more promises. Bill Sparrow carried her downstairs to look at the gerbil cage, quiet and safe, and then carried her back to bed. At last everyone was in bed again, free to sleep again.

But Peggy could not sleep.

Bill had shown Amy the gerbil cage, but the gerbils themselves had not been out. Peggy knew she was being over-anxious, but she wondered about them, worried about them. At last she crept out of bed and downstairs. There was still no sign of Bubble and Squeak. Not surprising, she knew. They must be deep in the hay nest in their bedroom. Ordinarily she would have left them undisturbed. But tonight – after the dustbin morning – she wanted to be sure. She opened the door of the cage, and put her hand in. Cautiously she moved aside the top hay in the bedroom. There was the brindle of gerbil fur, and it was warm to the touch. When she touched them, the gerbils fidgeted uneasily. She covered them up again quickly, shut the cage door and secured it, and went back upstairs.

At her own bedroom door, Peggy hesitated. She turned aside into Sid's room. She felt lonely, troubled.

She had not expected Sid to be still awake, and would not have woken him. But the slight noise she made in entering caused him to roll over creakily in bed. He whispered: 'Well, were they all right?'

'Bubble and Squeak? Yes. But I can't sleep.'

'Nor me.'

She sat down on the end of the bed and drew Sid's

eiderdown round her. 'But I'm not a bit worried about Bubble and Squeak,' she said.

'No?'

'Not now Mum's promised not to get rid of them.'

'Oh.'

'What do you mean – saying "Oh" like that, Sid?'

'I just said "Oh".'

'You didn't. You said it in a funny way.'

'Look, Peggy, I didn't ask you to come into my room in the middle of the night and keep me awake with silly talk. You go back to bed.'

She did not move. She repeated: 'Mum's promised not to get rid of Bubble and Squeak. A promise is a promise. She can't get out of that.'

Sid said: 'You'd be surprised . . .'

'Now what do you mean, Sid Parker?'

Sid said: 'Mum doesn't love my gerbils now any more than she did before. This morning she just about got them murdered –'

'No! She didn't – she didn't mean to! You heard what she said: she put them *on* the dustbin, not inside it.'

Sid said carefully: 'I don't think she really knew herself what she meant to happen. She was a bit off her head. She still is, a bit. All right: she promised. But she only needs some cast iron excuse . . .'

'A promise is a promise,' Peggy repeated.

'Look,' said Sid once more. 'I heard her this morning, talking to Bill. She said she was worrying about rabies. Whether you could catch rabies from a gerbil bite, because if so, really how *wrong* to keep gerbils at all. And when Bill said, No, he was sure you couldn't catch rabies from gerbils, she looked terribly – well, disappointed.'

He had convinced her of his point. She whispered: 'Then they really are still in danger. All the time here, there're in danger. Sid, this house isn't a safe place for them.'

Hard-voiced, Sid replied: 'They're my gerbils. Where I live, they live. I'm not going to let them go.'

'But, Sid, if you didn't give them away – if you just let them be out of this house for a bit – just for a bit, Sid – till Mum really gets used to the idea of having them – please, Sid – not far away, and not for long –'

'What are you driving at?'

'The Mudds would take them for a bit. I asked Dawn at school today. She's sure they would. They've only got Mrs Mudd's budgie and Mr Mudd's racing pigeons.'

'You really expect me to let my gerbils go to the Mudds?'

'Only for a little while – say, a week or two. Until we see that Mum feels better about them. Calmer.'

'No!'

'Please, Sid!'

'No!'

She was nearly crying. 'It's horrible of you! Just because they're your gerbils! But they're Bubble and Squeak, and they're in danger of their lives! You don't care! You don't love them!'

'Get out of my room!' said Sid in a low, savage whisper, 'Go on – get out!'

The next morning, even before they went downstairs to breakfast, Sid said to Peggy: 'Ask Dawn. Only for a week, mind. Or ten days at the outside.'

The arrangement was made easily enough.

Mrs Sparrow, when she heard of it, said nothing at all, but surely she could not have been displeased. Bill Sparrow said: 'Good old Dawn Mudd!'

The only one who questioned the gerbils' going away was Amy; and Sid and Peggy satisfied her by calling it a special holiday for Bubble and Squeak. Amy knew only one kind of special holiday; so she made seaside buckets and spades for Bubble and Squeak. The buckets were of paper, with cotton thread handles; the spades were of more paper, with matchstick handles. Amy pushed this equipment through the bars of the cage. Bubble and Squeak fell upon it greedily and gnawed it all to bits within a few minutes.

Amy, not minding at all about the buckets and spades, said, 'When will they come back from their special holiday with the Mudds?'

'A week on Sunday without fail,' said Peggy.

Mrs Sparrow had not seemed to be listening, but now she said, 'Perhaps the Mudds would like to keep them for good? If they're *very* happy there . . .'

'Oh, no,' Peggy said quickly. She glanced at Sid, but he was not taking part in this conversation. 'You see, there's the budgie, and Mr Mudd has his pigeons, and Dawn says her mother has a fur-allergy.'

'I don't see that pigeons and a budgie and two gerbils couldn't get on,' said Mrs Sparrow. 'They'd all be quite separate.'

'But then there's the fur-allergy.'

'Why couldn't the gerbils get on with this firaliji, if it's kept in a separate cage?'

'No, Mum, it's not an animal. It's a – a thing that Mrs Mudd's got.'

'I understood that perfectly well, thank you.'

'No, Mum: it's an allergy she's got – to fur. Fur brings on a kind of cold. Like hay-fever, rather.'

Mrs Sparrow drew a deep breath. 'I always thought she was a sly woman,' she said, and slammed off into the kitchen. She came back to say: 'And what the Council's thinking of – letting old man Mudd keep all those pigeons! It's a disgrace!'

This time she slammed off and did not come back.

CHAPTER 7

Mrs Sparrow had a delightful holiday from the gerbils.

On the first Saturday Bill Sparrow gave up his usual gardening and took his wife into town. They went shopping. They chose new curtain material for the living-room, and Bill Sparrow put down the money for it. Afterwards they had some tea, and then they went to the cinema.

The next day Mrs Sparrow spent some happy hours making up the new curtains. From the old curtains she made new cushion covers. From the old cushion covers she made new dusters. She already had a large number of dusters, but Mrs Sparrow did a good deal of dusting.

Meanwhile, the gerbils had settled into the Mudd household. The Mudds were easy people. Mr and Mrs Mudd had never bothered much with television or books or conversation: Mr Mudd was preoccupied with his pigeons; Mrs Mudd knitted. If Dawn wanted two gerbils in her room for a bit, that was all right. If her friend, Peggy Parker, wanted to stay for the night, while the gerbils were there, that was also all right. There was a put-you-up bed, and Peggy brought her own sleeping-bag.

It was also all right if Peggy's brother, Sid, came every day to attend to his gerbils. He had forbidden Peggy and Dawn to take the gerbils out of their cage except when he was there. He was afraid of some mishap in a strange house. But he came regularly to renew the gerbils' food and change their water, to give them a quick run, and to see them securely home again.

When Sid had gone, it was very quiet in the Mudds' house. The distant cooing of the pigeons from the bottom of the garden, the hymning of Mrs Mudd as she knitted downstairs – that was all. Peggy lowered her chin on to her arms, spread on the table in front of the gerbil cage, and stared at Bubble and Squeak. Bubble and Squeak stared back.

She wondered what it was like to see everything through bars, to have beneath your feet a little sawdust-covered metal floor instead of the vast Mongolian desert. To have bars above you, and above the bars a white ceiling, instead of blue infinity.

'I suppose it's their home,' she said aloud.

Dawn said, 'What is?'

'Their cage. They were born in this cage, or one just like it, at the Garden Centre. Their home. Just as our house is our home.'

'But they can't walk in and out, as you walk in and out of your house.'

'Sid lets them out.'

'Sid puts them back.'

'I go out of our house; I come back.'

'No,' said Dawn Mudd. 'It's not the same at all.' She thought carefully. 'At least, it's not quite the same.'

'Do they long and long to be free? I think they do. Sid thinks they don't, but that's because they're his gerbils. He wants them to want to stay his.'

'Nobody knows what gerbils long for, for certain,' said Dawn Mudd. 'But they wouldn't get peanuts anywhere but in that cage. That's for certain.'

They heard a hymn getting louder. Mrs Mudd was coming upstairs with a cup of cocoa and a mincepie each. It was weeks to Christmas yet; but, as she said, she liked to look ahead. (Mrs Mudd was knitting for an unborn grandchild: knitting needles stuck out now from the pocket of her overall.) These were the first mincepies of the season. So, wish.

Peggy looked at Bubble and Squeak, and took a first bite and wished.

Mrs Mudd did not come far into the room, or stay long, because of her fur-allergy. But she said to Peggy:

'Mr Mudd thought of taking some pigeon droppings round to your dad. That all right?'

'I should think so.'

As Mrs Mudd left them, she was plucking the needles from her pocket and resuming her carolling.

Through the bedroom window they saw Mr Mudd coming round the corner of the house from the direction of his pigeons in the back garden. From above, there wasn't much to be seen of him. Mr Mudd was smaller than Mrs Mudd. He was quite bald on the top of his head, with a little fringe of straight red hair round the baldness. Just now he was carrying a bucket of pigeon droppings. People on the estate who were favoured with Mudd droppings grew by far the best dahlias. Mr Mudd went off in the direction of Bill Sparrow and his garden.

Dawn Mudd said: 'Do you remember your dad?'

'You mean my real dad? David Parker?'

'Was his name David? What was he like?'

'I – I don't know. But if I saw him, I'd know him.'

'But he's dead!'

'Yes. But I'd know him.'

'Was he nicer than Bill Sparrow?'

'Yes. Well, really, I suppose I just don't know. Bill's not bad. My real dad – I remember he used to give me his finger to hold, instead of his hand. I used to take hold of it with the whole of my hand, and we'd walk along – like hand in hand, only finger in hand. He had a big finger, and I had a little hand then. My hand's much bigger now.' Peggy held her hand in front of her, turned it. She brooded. 'Sid remembers him properly. Amy doesn't remember him at all.'

Dawn said: 'Funny.'

'Funny?'

'I was just trying to imagine someone who wasn't my dad being my dad . . . Just funny.'

Mr Mudd had disappeared round a far corner.

They both fell into silence. Distantly pigeons cooed. From downstairs Mrs Mudd changed her tune: *O come, all ye faithful!* she sang, joyfully and triumphantly.

Dawn Mudd said: 'I saw a book in the Library: *How to enjoy gerbils*. I got it out. I thought it might be good for your mum.'

Peggy said: 'She'd never, never read it.'

But Dawn Mudd had not been so silly as to expect that. 'I thought, just leave it about in your house, where she'll see it. There are lots of coloured pictures. She might pick it up, just to look at the pictures. Then read a bit, perhaps.'

'All right. I'll try.'

So Peggy took home with her that day the book called *How to enjoy gerbils* and laid it on the living-room table, open. Bill Sparrow saw it there, picked it up, and spent some time looking through it. He put it back, closed, with the front cover uppermost, on the table again.

Mrs Sparrow came in and saw the book. '*How to enjoy gerbils*,' she read. On the last word she gave a snort and flung the book, unopened, on to a chair. Later, however, she moved the book again, and in doing so she opened it. She began to read a little. Sid walked in as she was reading.

'Sid, how old are those gerbils of yours?'

'Jimmy Dean's cousin said one. About one.'

'So they've probably another one to three more years of life before them?'

'I don't know. Perhaps.'

'So it says here. Well, isn't that nice for me? Only three more years, at the outside, to have to endure them!'

She slapped the book down yet again and walked out of the room. She passed Peggy in the doorway.

'She was reading it, wasn't she?' Peggy asked eagerly.

'She may never actually *enjoy* gerbils,' said Sid, 'but at least she's facing up to them.'

CHAPTER 8

The gerbils came home from the Mudds' house in the last week before the Christmas holidays.

They were received with rejoicing by the children. Bill Sparrow looked on, smiling. Their mother held aloof, but there seemed no doubt that she did not feel as badly about gerbils as she had once done. She put up with them. She did not love them – any more than she loved other things she had to put up with. She put up with the draught through the back door, and old Mrs Pring's cats, and Bill Sparrow's gardening boots. She loved none of these things, but she put up with them. Now she had begun putting up with gerbils.

On the first morning after the gerbils' return, Peter Peters called early on the way to school. He wanted to see Bubble and Squeak again. Peggy left her breakfast, in the middle, to show them to him. Amy had finished her breakfast and went with her. Then Peggy came back to the kitchen, leaving Amy and Peter Peters gazing into the gerbil cage.

'Did you tell them not to take them out?' Sid asked. Peggy called to Amy from the kitchen with Sid's message.

Peggy and Sid went on with their breakfasts. Bill had nearly finished his. Mrs Sparrow was busy about the kitchen.

Amy and Peter Peters were still with the gerbils.

Dawn Mudd called. That meant it was time to set off for school.

'Come on, Amy!' her mother called. 'Or you'll be late!'

What happened next is not certain, because neither Amy nor Peter Peters were reliable witnesses. What is certain is that, disobeying Sid, Amy had taken either Bubble or Squeak out to show Peter Peters. They were stroking the gerbil when Mrs Sparrow called from the kitchen. Amy was instantly in a hurry not to be late. The gerbil was put back into the cage at once. Then, at once, Amy shut the door of the cage, and slammed the bolt across it. The bolt was made of wire, and rather light: it had to be shot home rather carefully, and Amy was in too much of a hurry to be careful. Either she did not shoot the bolt far enough, or she shot it so hard that it bounced back. Whichever happened, the door of the cage came ajar.

The enterprising gerbils took advantage of this.

The one lucky thing, as Bill Sparrow later pointed out, was that they must have escaped almost at once. They began exploring. Already Peggy and Amy, with Dawn Mudd and Peter Peters, had left for school; but the others were still in the kitchen. The door from the hall into the kitchen was open, like the door from the living-room into the hall. Mrs Sparrow, facing in that direction, gave a moan. Bill was half-way through his last cup of tea; Sid was tying his shoe-laces. Both looked up, and turned towards the point at which Mrs Sparrow was staring.

On the threshold of the doorway sat Bubble – or was it Squeak? He sat up on his haunches, his forepaws against his chest, gazing at them all in amazement.

Sid pushed his chair back with a cry, and Bill Sparrow gave a sudden guffaw.

Squeak – or was it Bubble? – dropped suddenly on all fours, and whisked round the corner and back in the direction from which he must have come.

Sid rushed after him.

There was no sign of a gerbil in the hall by the time Sid got there, nor on the living-room floor. However, a gerbil was perched on the cushion of a chair within easy jumping distance of the top of the living-room table. That gerbil somehow looked as if it had just come from the table, not as if it were in the act of going back to it. But, of course, you couldn't be sure. Unless you were Peggy, you simply could not be sure which gerbil was which.

On the living-room table stood the cage, empty, of course, and with its door wide open.

One gerbil, but not two.

Sid made a quick dive towards the gerbil on the cushion. The gerbil made a quick dive into the narrow dark cavern formed by the leaning of the cushion against the back of the chair.

'Got you!' said Sid. He began exploring with one hand from one side of the cushion and with the other from the other. His hands met: no gerbil. The gerbil popped out suddenly from underneath the middle of the cushion. Sid whipped one hand out to catch him. His fingers closed on him, but roughly. The gerbil bit him. Sid yelped and let go. The gerbil darted back under the cushion.

'Want help?' asked Bill. He had followed Sid at leisure.

'Put in one hand here, and the other hand the other side,' directed Sid. 'And don't try to catch him with your whole hand. He's in a panic. He'll bite. Get his tail. But, anyway, he'll probably come out at the front again, and I'll catch him then.'

Bill Sparrow did as he was told. As before, the gerbil came out at the front of the cushion, where Sid was waiting for him. Sid pounced more skilfully this time, caught him by his tail, and popped him into the cage. He shut the door and bolted it carefully.

One gerbil – but not two.

His mother stood behind him. 'It's time to go. Have you got it?'

'Yes. One. But not both.'

'For Heaven's sake! A gerbil loose, and we're both going to be late for work, and you're going to miss your school bus!' She began frantically moving chairs and also cushions on chairs. The other two searched as well.

No second gerbil.

Mrs Sparrow glanced at the clock. 'You go, Bill. I'll follow.

He went.

She eyed her son. 'I'm not going until I've seen you on that bus, Sid.'

Plainly she meant what she said. So Sid decided to be plain with his mother, too. 'I'm not going to school until I've found my gerbil. If it's left to itself all day, anything might happen.'

'What?'

'If it got outside somehow, a cat.'

Mrs Sparrow said nothing.

'Or it could get under the floorboards and die of starvation there. And rot. And smell.'

Sid was watching his mother closely. Her expression was changing from its original firmness.

'Under the floorboards?'

'Yes.'

Suddenly she said: 'Promise me faithfully that, if you do find it by dinner-time, you'll go in to afternoon school. I'll give you money for the bus fare.'

He promised.

'Although what reason you'll give for not going this morning . . .'

'I could tell them the truth.'

Just as Mrs Sparrow was leaving the house, she stuck her head in again: 'I'll tell Mrs Pring. She'll look in to see you're all right. And you can help yourself from the fridge.'

When his mother had gone, Sid did a thorough turn out of the living-room. Somehow it looked tousled when he had finished with it. No gerbil.

But he supposed that the gerbil might have gone anywhere, even upstairs. So upstairs and downstairs Sid searched, wherever a door had been left ajar, or wherever there was a gap between the bottom of a shut door and the threshold (and the house was not a particularly well-built one). Soon most of the house began to have that tousled look.

But no gerbil.

He wondered if it were true that gerbils come back to their home cages in the end, anyway. He would have to rely on that, or on the gerbil's moving about enough to make a noise he could hear. He himself would have to be very quiet.

He took a comfortable chair out into the hall, where he hoped to be able to hear a sound – if it were loud enough – from anywhere in the house. Luckily the caged gerbil seemed asleep, so there was no noise from *him*. But Sid heard his own noises, as he fidgeted anxiously in his chair. The creak of the chair . . . the scrape of his shoe against the leg . . . and then his own breathing . . . and a cough he would have to let out . . .

But the house round him was so still that he jumped when the flap of the front door letterbox went up. He guessed it was old Mrs Pring. So it was dinner-time already.

Mrs Pring always thought of Sid as a little boy, because she had known him so long. She called through the letterbox: 'Don't be frightened, dear. I've brought you some hot soup, and I thought I'd bring you –' On the last word, her fingers must have slipped, for the word was lost in the clatter of the flap snapping down again.

Sid could see through the glass panels of the front door that the dumpy figure of Mrs Pring was burdened with two objects. One – the bowl of soup? – in her right hand; the other, a light orangey-brown colour, on or under her left arm. No wonder she hadn't managed to keep the letter-flap up for long.

Unsuspecting, Sid threw wide the front door.

In her right hand Mrs Pring carried a steaming bowl.

Under her left arm she carried her cat, Ginger.

Sid gaped at the cat, while Mrs Pring began at once to say that his mother had said there was a rat in the house, and that Sid was trying to catch it, and if so, Ginger was the one. The best ratter, the best mouser –

All the time, Mrs Pring was advancing into the house.

Sid came to life. 'No!' he cried, realizing that this was not the time for politeness. But he was already too late.

Ginger – like most cats – did not like being carried for long. He had begun to wriggle, and Mrs Pring was not one to oppose her cat's wishes. She allowed Ginger to leap from her arms. He began walking down the hall towards the living-room. Sid tried to catch him. Ginger accelerated his pace just enough to escape from under Sid's hands and into the living-room. At that moment, the gerbil already in the cage decided to get out of bed. He rustled through the hay of his bedroom – and Ginger at once froze.

The gerbil moved into sight at the bars of his cage, and Ginger was crouching lower – lower – like a snake against the ground, still except for the tip of his tail, which flicked to and fro . . .

Although Sid knew that the gerbil was protected by its cage, he threw himself upon Ginger before the leap. This time he caught the cat and held him long enough to open the window and fling him out.

Ginger landed neatly on all four paws, but was displeased – one could see that. He sat down at once and began cleaning himself, as though he had never really meant to go gerbil-hunting. What he had always really intended was to clean himself in the fresh air.

Sid shut the window again, and had to face Mrs Pring.

Mrs Pring was even more offended than Ginger. She put the soup down carefully on the kitchen table and then scolded Sid like a very little boy. She said that all children should know about kindness to animals, and Ginger was such a kind cat that he should never have been thrown anywhere, let alone out of a window. He would have caught that horrid rat for Sid, wherever it had hidden itself in the house . . .

'Yes, Mrs Pring, yes,' murmured Sid.

In the end, Mrs Pring went, and Sid drank his soup in the kitchen, and made himself a cheese-and-pickle sandwich, and ate it as he sat in the hall. He began eating an apple, but found the crunching sound deafening. You couldn't listen for gerbil-noises through all that row.

He sat with the doors of the living-room and cloakroom open; also all the doors upstairs. He was giving himself the best chance of hearing any unusual sound in the house. He could also see most of the hall, and into the cloakroom and the living-room. He could even see the gerbil cage on the table in the living-room. He couldn't see the gerbil inside: it must be having its afternoon nap in its hay bed.

After a while, from the living-room, he heard the gentle little scrabbling-gnawing sound of a gerbil awake and active. In his mind, he set the sound to one side, and went on listening for the special sound of an escaped gerbil. He glanced into the living-room: still no sign of the gerbil in the cage.

Then he woke up to what that might mean.

He rose from his chair and went softly into the living-room and bent over the cage. The gerbil was buried in the hay of its bedroom. It stirred a little, as he looked, but certainly not enough to account for the sound he had heard.

Besides – there was the sound again, and it didn't come from the cage at all, but from the other side of the room. He stood absolutely still and listened. Yes, again; and from the far side of the room.

He went over on tiptoe; but, as soon as he moved, the noise stopped. They had looked behind the furniture here, and found nothing; but perhaps . . .

Suddenly, the noise again. He found that his gaze had fixed itself upon the edge of the carpet, where it met the wall. Only it wasn't exactly an edge there. Years ago Mrs Sparrow had bought the carpet second-hand. It was rather too long for the living-room, but she had not liked to cut it to size. So one end of it had been folded under. The fold of the carpet where it reached the wall made the longest, darkest, most tempting tunnel that either Bubble or Squeak could have wished for, outside Mongolia.

Sid knew in his bones that the escaped gerbil was in the carpet-tunnel.

His impulse was to rush forward, flap the carpet back, and catch the gerbil. Catch the gerbil? He found that he was trembling: he was terribly afraid that he would somehow mess it all up, and the gerbil would escape again, and get more and more panicky, and he would get more and more excited, and he would never catch his gerbil . . .

He decided what to do. He got two of the largest pieces of coal from the scuttle, and weighed down either end of the carpet-tunnel. He checked that the two exits were really closed. Of course, any gerbil worth his salt could gnaw his way through a wall of carpet, but that would take a little time. Meanwhile, Sid dashed upstairs to the bathroom and brought down the empty laundry box. It was really just a deep box, standing on four legs, with a hinged lid. At each side, near the top, was a hand-hole, so that one could carry the box easily. These hand-holes would ventilate the box, when the lid was down. Here was a very simple gerbil container. He felt sure that, if only he could catch the gerbil, he could drop it into this box. If he tried to get it through the narrow cage door straight into the cage – well, he didn't trust himself. The other gerbil might be trying to get out, or he might drop this one. Or anything might happen.

It was extraordinary how nervous he felt.

He padded the bottom of the laundry box with a scarlet cushion, and left the lid up. He drew the box as near to the carpet-fold as possible. He removed the lump of coal from one end of the tunnel.

He was ready.

But there was no sound at all now from inside the tunnel. He realized that there had been no sound since he had come back from the bathroom with the box. Perhaps the gerbil had already escaped from the carpet-fold. He was almost sure that must be so. Yes, he was convinced of it. On an impulse of despair, he seized the corner of the carpet and flapped back the fold.

There was the gerbil.

Forgetting all about the wisdom of picking up a gerbil by its tail, he clapped his hands over it quickly, roughly. The gerbil bit him, but he hardly noticed.

Down into the laundry box, and slam the lid!

He had his gerbil. He had them both – Bubble and Squeak.

He laughed aloud. The thought of school never occurred to him – and indeed it was much too late for that, anyway. He began to dance, like a teetotum. Faster and faster, round and round, laughing. He stopped only when he found himself staggering about the room, giddy. He stopped, and fell crazily on the couch. His head was rocking. He lay with closed eyes. His mind became delightfully muddled.

He slept.

When the others came home, they found him asleep on the couch, and the gerbil – it was Squeak, Peggy said – safe in the laundry box. It had gnawn a hole in the scarlet cushion cover and down into the stuffing of the cushion. That was all.

Everyone was pleased at the happy end of the story. Sid hardly scolded Amy. Even Mrs Sparrow, looking at the gnawn cushion cover, only said: 'Well, you can't have too many dusters.'

But that wasn't really the end of the story.

By now it was quite dark outside, so that no one in the house noticed someone outside, peering in: Ginger. The house held a fascination for him.

CHAPTER 9

So suddenly does disaster strike.

That evening Bill Sparrow had gone to get more coal for the fire.

'Shut the back door – the draught's killing!' called Mrs Sparrow. But, as usual, Bill did not shut the door – it would be so much easier to find it open when he came back, laden with coal. He pulled the back door to, but did not click it shut. It opened a little behind him as he turned away. He went off with the scuttle towards the coal-bunker.

Behind him a ginger ghost slipped up to the back door, and through it, into the house.

Ginger went through the kitchen and across the hall into the living-room. Bill Sparrow had left all those doors ajar for his return.

Once inside the living-room, Ginger melted into the shadows. The whole family were watching television. Everyone was staring, silent, in one direction. The electric light had been switched off. The fire had burnt low, but there was a cold glow from the television screen. In the light Ginger's eyes shone large, but no one saw them.

He had not chosen his time particularly well. The gerbils might so easily have been at exercise on the living-room table; but they were safely in their cage.

So at first Ginger saw nothing of particular interest. The television screen did not interest him, nor the sounds that proceeded from the set. There were gun-shots, screams, alarm-bells and sirens: Ginger paid no attention.

But then there was another sound: a little scuffling and scratching, and a subdued *Creak! . . . Creak! . . . Creak!* Nobody looking at the television screen even turned a head: they were used to the fidgetings of Bubble and Squeak by now.

But the ginger ghost in the shadows began to move. From shadow to shadow he slipped, round the back of the chairs and the couch, until he was close to the table.

From inside their cage on the table the gerbils saw him. They froze.

Ginger saw them and leapt . . .

The television viewers were aware of something that

hurtled through the air, and an impact like an explosion. That was Ginger reaching the cage. Suddenly everyone was shouting or shrieking. The cage skidded off the table and on to the floor with a crash. The whole of the barred side and roof flew off in one piece. The two gerbils leapt for their lives.

Peggy saw one gerbil and dived for it and caught it.

Ginger saw the other gerbil – Bubble – and dived for it and caught it.

Peggy was screaming because, holding one gerbil, she could do nothing about the other one. Sid was yelling because he was trying to frighten Ginger into dropping his prey. Amy was screaming, anyway. But Mrs Sparrow was not screaming. She was the only one within reach of Ginger and Bubble, and she was inspired. She flung herself forward on to Ginger's tail, gripped it, held it with both hands, hauled on it.

Ginger turned on Mrs Sparrow. He scratched her viciously: she still held on. Suddenly what was happening to him was too much to be borne – Ginger was no hero. He wanted to yowl, and he opened his mouth and yowled. A sad little bundle of fur, brindled and white, fell from his jaws. Sid saw it, darted in and picked it up.

Mrs Sparrow let go of Ginger's tail. Ginger sprang for the door – out, and across the hall and kitchen and out through the back door just as Bill Sparrow was coming in with the coal. As only a cat can, Ginger slipped between Bill's legs so that he tottered and fell, with a scuttleful of coal and a great deal of swearing.

Coal all over the kitchen floor.

Mrs Sparrow scratched quite badly.

Amy almost in hysterics.

And Bubble – 'Is he all right?' whispered Peggy.

'Just,' said Sid.

Bill Sparrow had left coal all over the kitchen floor and come in to see what on earth had been happening. He made his wife sit down. He switched off the television set. He reassembled the gerbil cage so that Peggy could put Squeak back. He took Amy into his arms. Then he looked at Bubble, held cupped in Sid's hands. He looked long, and then he cleared his throat. 'I had a white mouse. A cat mauled it. The mouse had to be put out of its misery. It was kinder. It had to be destroyed . . .'

From her chair, Mrs Sparrow, hearing him, groaned.

CHAPTER 10

Sid maintained that Bubble was hardly hurt at all. He was suffering only from shock, Sid said. He had had a terrifying experience, in the very jaws of a cat, and he had been shocked by it. No worse than that. Back in the cage with Squeak, Bubble had behaved almost normally. He had even drunk a good deal of water.

But, the next day, Bubble was ill. And the day after that he was worse. He hunched up small, hardly moving. When he did move, he turned distractedly in circles.

Bill Sparrow said grimly: 'Sid, you're being cruel.'

At that, Peggy wept. Dawn Mudd had no consolation to offer.

Mrs Sparrow took Amy with her to the shops.

And Sid said: 'I'm going to take him to the vet.' Peggy would go too.

The Christmas holidays had begun, so there was no problem of time. They prepared a vehicle for Bubble: an old biscuit tin with holes in the top for ventilation, and plenty of old newspaper at the bottom, and hay. They put in some toilet-roll tubes, but Bubble was past caring to gnaw anything – or to eat anything. Perhaps past caring to live.

They travelled to the vet by bus, sitting side by side. They did not often do things together: Sid had his friends, Peggy had hers. Peggy thought: 'Perhaps when I'm old, I shall remember this bus ride.' Then she thought that, when she was old, Bubble would be long dead, anyway. Tears of hopelessness rolled down her cheeks.

Sid had been watching the passengers reflected in the glass of the bus window. He watched Peggy. He did not turn his head towards her, but his hand picked up her hand and gripped it.

They had never been in a vet's surgery before – they had never had a pet before. In the waiting-room a number of people sat around in silence with their pets, who all seemed enormous to Peggy and Sid. Everyone stared at their tin with holes in the top; no one spoke to them. There were two cats in cat baskets but they both stayed asleep. A scruffy little black dog, wearing a red plastic bucket like a bonnet, to keep it from scratching a bad eye, came bustling up to them. But 'Flora!' said a stern voice, and she went away again.

They were called into the surgery itself, and opened their box, and told their story. The vet picked up poor Bubble, hardly struggling, by his tail. He turned him round and round, parted his fur here and there with a finger. He asked when the attack had happened.

'The day before yesterday,' said Sid. 'We thought he might just get better. But he hasn't.'

'He's got much worse,' said Peggy.

The vet put Bubble down on his black-topped table and watched him. He stirred him gently, and Bubble began his distracted circling.

'Please don't worry him,' said Peggy. The tears rolled down her cheeks.

The vet did not answer.

Then he said: 'I think his wounds are only puncture wounds, from the cat's teeth holding him. But there's infection. Bad, very bad.'

He looked at them both, especially Peggy, crying. He said gently: 'Would you like to leave him with me?'

'Oh, yes,' cried Peggy joyfully, not understanding.

But Sid, seeing that the vet had more to say, but hesitated to say it, asked: 'For how long?'

'For good.' The vet cleared his throat, as Bill Sparrow had done. 'You see –' But Peggy had already begun to sob.

'Is there nothing we can do?' Sid asked.

'It's probably too late; but I suppose you could try an

antibiotic. It would be touch and go; and very tricky for you. Very tricky.'

'We'll try the antibiotic.'

The vet gave them a little plastic syringe; also some white powder in a sealed envelope. He explained how they must dissolve a pinch of the powder in a measure of water, fill the syringe with it, and then pump three or four drops of the solution into Bubble's mouth. This had to be done three times a day.

'The tricky part will be getting him to take it,' said the vet. He showed them what to do. It needed two people. One held the gerbil by his tail on the table, and had the filled syringe ready. The other had to hold the gerbil's head steady and up. That meant gripping it by the skin at the back of the head. The vet showed them. It seemed quite easy when he showed them.

Then they shut Bubble into his travelling box, and they paid the vet – they had been given money by Bill Sparrow. To Mrs Sparrow it would have seemed a great deal of money for a creature not a human being, and a very small creature at that.

As they were leaving the surgery, Sid asked: 'How long will the treatment take?'

'Give it a week. Try it.' And then: 'I'm afraid his chances of survival are poor. Very poor.'

At home that evening the first dose had to be given. Sid and Peggy were to do it on the living-room table. They waited until Amy had been put to bed. Then Mrs Sparrow deliberately busied herself in the kitchen. Bill Sparrow deliberately busied himself with the evening paper. It was going to be tricky, the vet had said.

Squeak watched through the bars of his cage with bulging eyes.

Sid brought Bubble out by his tail and set him on the table. He hardly moved of his own accord, and was so thin that he seemed to have shrunk to half Squeak's size. You could see the tiny knobbles of his backbone through his fur.

Sid held Bubble's tail by his left hand; in his right he had the filled syringe. 'Ready?' he asked Peggy.

'Yes.' With index finger and thumb she took up a pinch of skin just at the back of the gerbil's head. This seemed to be as the vet had instructed, but her grip slipped at once. The gerbil's head went down and sideways, and he was feebly attempting to escape.

'Try again,' said Sid.

Again, this time so carefully that she missed her grip altogether.

'Again,' said Sid grimly. He was determined to get some drops in from the syringe if there were any chance at all. He held the syringe close to Bubble's jaws.

Peggy's finger and thumb came down again. The gerbil gave a tiny, weak sound like a gerbil scream. She had him, but not by the skin of his head – much lower. Sid tried to get the nozzle of the syringe between his teeth, but it was hopeless. The tiny head moved frantically. The health-giving drops seemed to go everywhere but into the gerbil's mouth.

Peggy let Bubble go and burst into tears. Sid lifted him by his tail and put him back into his hay. Then he sat down at the table again. He was trembling.

Mrs Sparrow came in from the kitchen. 'Have you finished?'

'No,' said Bill Sparrow.

Peggy wept and wept. 'I can't – I can't!'

Sid said stonily, 'He'll die if you don't. But he'll probably die, anyway.'

Bill said: 'I'd have a go, but –' He spread out the fingers of his hand. They were so much too big for any job like that.

Peggy sobbed: 'I'll go and fetch Dawn.'

Mrs Sparrow said, 'You'll do no such thing. Show me, Sid.'

Peggy hushed suddenly. Bill Sparrow put his newspaper away.

Sid got Bubble out again and showed his mother where her grip should be. 'Right!' said Mrs Sparrow. She had never touched one of the gerbils before, but now all her mind and will concentrated on taking hold of this one.

'Ready?' asked Sid. He held the syringe as close as he could.

'Ready.'

'Right, then!'

Mrs Sparrow's finger and thumb plummeted down to grip in exactly the right place; but then – like Peggy's – they slid sideways. The gerbil squirmed from her. As he did so, a pinch of fur came off between

Mrs Sparrow's finger-tip and thumb-tip. 'Aaargh!' she muttered – the only time she expressed distaste. Then: 'Keep hold of his tail, Sid,' she said. 'I'm going to try again.'

This time her grip was quick, accurate and firm: she held the gerbil's head steadily up, and Sid pumped between its teeth the necessary drops.

'Right,' said Sid.

'Right,' said his mother.

Sid lifted Bubble back into his hay. He checked the time on his watch. Bubble would need another three drops tomorrow morning before breakfast; another three at dinner time; a last lot in the evening.

'Lucky I'm working half-time for holidays,' Mrs Sparrow said.

The day on which Bubble twisted round energetically in Mrs Sparrow's grip and tried to bite her, Sid cried: 'He's better – he's really better!'

That evening he ate a peanut.

The next day he gnawed at a toilet-roll tube.

Meanwhile, Bill Sparrow had made another gerbil cage – a bit rough looking, but all right – for Bubble. For it seemed hard that an invalid should have to share with the energetic Squeak.

The children were watching Bubble through the bars of the new cage early one evening. They were waiting for Bill Sparrow to get home: he was unusually late. When he came, they would have tea. After tea, Mrs Sparrow would be free to help with the antibiotic treatment, which had to continue for only a little longer.

The front door bell rang, and Mrs Sparrow went to answer it.

A boy whom – to her remembrance – she had never seen before stood on the doorstep. He was about Sid's age, or younger; but he was small – small in every way, except for his eyes. His eyes were large, and they fixed themselves intently upon Mrs Sparrow's face.

'Please,' he said, 'I'm Jimmy Dean's cousin. We've come back from Australia. It didn't suit. Please, I'd like my gerbils back again.'

CHAPTER 11

Mrs Sparrow's first impulse was to slam the door in Jimmy Dean's cousin's face. Instead, she said, 'You'd better come in and speak to Sid.'

Jimmy Dean's cousin followed her along the hall and into the living-room.

Sid recognized him as soon as he walked in. 'You've come for the gerbils you gave me,' he said. Peggy gasped.

'Yes,' said Jimmy Dean's cousin. His eyes had settled instantly on the two cages on the table. 'Why've you separated them?' he asked angrily. He was a small-sized boy, but he seemed to swell with indignation. He fumbled in his pocket, brought out some pound notes, and slapped them on the table. 'There you are!' he said. 'I wasn't expecting my gerbils back as a gift. I'm buying them back, with their cage. At once. Didn't you even know that gerbils love each other's company?'

'One of them's been ill,' said Sid. 'Very ill.' They told Jimmy Dean's cousin the story of Ginger's attack. In the middle of the story, Mrs Sparrow said to him, 'Sit down and be comfortable, do'; and Amy offered him a peppermint. He sat down and took the peppermint, and he was now listening quite calmly to all that Sid had to say. But the pound notes remained on the table.

'So you see,' Sid ended, 'we can't very well hand you back a gerbil that's only just convalescent. In fact, he may never be completely fit, the vet says. He enjoys his food; but he seems to be deaf.'

'You know how to treat him, you should keep him,' said Jimmy Dean's cousin sadly.

'If we keep Bubble,' said Sid, 'we ought to keep Squeak – for *their* sakes. They enjoy each other's company, just as you said.'

'Yes, I see that,' said Jimmy Dean's cousin, even more sadly. He began picking up his pound notes and putting them away.

'They're going to be put together in one cage again, very soon,' said Peggy. 'As soon as Bubble seems strong enough for rough-and-tumble. Then there'll be a cage to spare.'

'You can have your very own cage back again,' said Sid. 'Free. A gift returned.'

'And you've got enough money to go to the Garden Centre and buy two more gerbils of your own.'

'Yes,' said Jimmy Dean's cousin. It seemed impossible for him to be sadder. Sid and Peggy and Mrs Sparrow looked at each other in dismay. It was awful to send him away feeling like that.

'Stay and have tea with us,' said Mrs Sparrow.

'No, thank you very much,' said Jimmy Dean's cousin. 'No.'

'Do stay!'

But it was Amy who made everything all right. She said wistfully: 'I wish we were having more gerbils. Then we could have a mum gerbil and a dad gerbil, and they'd have lots and lots of baby gerbils. Babies!'

Peggy was suddenly excited. 'That's what you can do,' she cried to Jimmy Dean's cousin. 'Make sure you buy two gerbils of opposite sex! Let them mate! Let them have babies!'

'Babies! Babies! Babies!' cried Amy.

Jimmy Dean's cousin was very much taken with the idea. 'But I don't know what my mum and dad would say,' he said.

'Pooh!' said Mrs Sparrow. 'They'll just have to put up with it, won't they?'

So, after all, Jimmy Dean's cousin decided to stay and have tea. He took off his anorak and settled down. He helped Sid administer the very nearly last dose of antibiotic to Bubble. Sid congratulated him on the steadiness of his hand, in doing what Mrs Sparrow usually had to do. Then, with Peggy, they took Squeak out of his cage on to the table and gave him a run in and out of newspaper tubes and cardboard tubes.

Meanwhile, Mrs Sparrow was in the kitchen, preparing something special for tea. From the living-room they could hear the spitting of fat in the pan and smell the delicious smell of sausages beginning to cook, and other frying.

Amy wandered between the kitchen and the living-room and back again. She seemed upset about something; but nobody felt they had to pay much attention.

The front gate clicked, which meant that Bill Sparrow was home at last. He shouted to them from outside: 'Someone come out and help me!' He did not sound in distress.

They all rushed out, and there he was struggling with a Christmas tree which he had brought home on his bicycle. He had had to push the bicycle, on foot. That was why he was so late home.

Now that she knew that nothing had gone wrong, Mrs Sparrow went back to her frying. Sid and Peggy and Jimmy Dean's cousin carried the Christmas tree indoors and propped it up for the time being in the usual corner of the living-room.

Only Amy was left outside with Bill Sparrow. Now that everyone else was gone, she had him to herself. She began crying.

Bill Sparrow put his bicycle away, and picked her up, and carried her indoors. 'What is it, then, lovey?'

'Bill! I think they're going to eat them!'

'Eat them?'

'Eat Bubble and Squeak for tea. Mum says so. Sid's pleased.'

'Are they now?' said Bill Sparrow. 'We'll have to sort that out, shan't we? I don't want fried gerbil for my tea!'

'Oh, *no*!'

He carried Amy into the kitchen and set her down there, calling to the other children as he did so. He said that he had brought presents home with him. They crowded in, with Jimmy Dean's cousin. Bill Sparrow said: 'The same present for everyone. I brought one for you, too, Alice; but perhaps I'd better give it to the young chap.' He nodded towards Jimmy Dean's cousin. 'Perhaps you won't mind not having yours, anyway, Alice.' He grinned. 'It's a white mouse each.'

'Bill!' She thought he must be joking.

But Bill Sparrow said, 'Yes. Really!'

Mrs Sparrow backed slowly into a corner of the kitchen, holding her cooking fork in front of her.

'Yes.' He dived a hand into a pocket and brought out a brown paper bag. It seemed an odd, unsafe way to carry four white mice, but he held the bag carefully and firmly as though he knew they might attempt to escape. Then he put a hand in: 'Ow!' he said, twisting his features. 'One bit!'

They all watched him, breathless, except for Mrs Sparrow, who had closed her eyes. She opened them in time to see him bring the first mouse out of the paper bag. He held it up by its tail – a white string tail for a white sugar mouse.

'Sugar mice!' Mrs Sparrow gave a wild screech of laughter that drowned everyone else's. They calmed her down; and Sid said, 'That was a really *good* joke.'

Then they all sat down to bubble-and-squeak with their tea. Bill explained to Amy, and she said happily: 'Not Bubble and Squeak. *Never* dear Bubble and Squeak.'

PHILIPPA PEARCE

Winner of the Carnegie Medal

Tom's Midnight Garden

Discover a place where magic starts to happen when the clock strikes 13 . . .

'Will send a tingle down your spine' – *Guardian*

'A masterpiece' – *Observer*

'Dreamy' – *Daily Express*

puffin.co.uk

Illustration © Jamel Akib

PHILIPPA PEARCE

Author of *Tom's Midnight Garden*

Winner of the Whitbread Children's Book Award

'Did you expect a *real* dog?'

Can you *really* make a picture of a dog come to life?

Ben's imagination can make anything happen . . .

a dog so small

'No writer captures the dreamy intensity of childhood better' – *Guardian*

puffin.co.uk

The Little Gentleman

PHILIPPA PEARCE

The award-winning author of *Tom's Midnight Garden*

'They were friends together, determined between them to achieve something heroic in the name of friendship'

Even the most unlikely friends can make your deepest, most secret wishes come true.

'Terrific' – *Sunday Times*

'A rare treat' – *Sunday Telegraph*

'Extraordinary' – *Daily Mail*

puffin.co.uk

Dick King-Smith

No. 1 for animal magic!

'Why can't I learn to be a sheep-pig?'

Babe wants to learn everything he needs to know to be a sheep-dog. He knows he can't be a real sheep-dog. But maybe, just maybe, he might be a sheep-PIG!

'A thrilling, funny, charmer of a book'
– *Guardian*

'Dick King-Smith is a huge favourite'
– *Observer*

Illustration © Chris Riddell